H. Scott R. Blake,

with Auntie Eva's

love.

# If I were King George

HAPPY

*From a Drawing by A. C. Michael*

# If I were King George

## by

# Happy

## The King's Dog

"Tout comprendre, c'est tout pardonner."

Hodder & Stoughton

*To*
*My* KING AND QUEEN
*They'll understand*
HAPPY

"Now then, out of the way, old sobersided Stick-in-the-mud," I barked. "I do wish you'd get it into that melancholy old head of yours that *I'm* the King's dog now and that you're not wanted here, moping about the Palace with your watery eyes and twisted mouth.

"That's right, put your ragged stumpy tail between your legs and slink away. It's *my* Palace

9

now. I'm as happy as a King—
I'm Happy, the King's dog."

"Quiet!" said King George.
"Lie down at once, Happy.
You don't understand."

Something in the King's voice
made Cæsar turn his head as he
mouched towards the door.

I growled.

It's rather fun quarrelling
with old Cæsar now. He used
to be a great fighter, not exactly
a dog to take liberties with I can
tell you, but in these last days
he doesn't seem to care, and
though he bares his teeth now

and again and mumbles away in his throat when we worry him, he's no spirit for a good set-to fight, and I must admit we all enjoy bullying him a bit.

I really wasn't in the least angry with Cæsar. I really didn't mean anything serious by growling, but to my surprise King George seemed most annoyed with me.

"Outside, Happy! Now! at once!" said he sharply.

And I went, very slowly and proudly of course, dragging one

leg stiffly after the other, as if it had just occurred to me that it might be interesting to see what they were doing in the passage.

As I passed through the door I heard King George say:

"Here, Cæsar! Poor old boy. Don't take any notice of him. *He doesn't understand.*"

Later in the day I went for a walk with King George. Or rather he went for a walk and I followed. He called me quite nicely as he was going out, but seeing the way he had treated me I didn't hurry, though I just longed for a mad scamper. I was in a regular temper, you know; I'd refused my dinner and was shivering all over with rage and hunger, oh! and with all kinds of wickedness.

I slouched along behind him, my ears well back, pretending not to care a — well, not a little bit.

The worst of it is I'm no good at pretending. I've asked several of my friends, and they say they're just the same. I wanted to look haughty and independent and don't-care-a-little-bittish, but I couldn't.

King George took no notice of me till we had gone some way from the Palace, and naturally I tried to take no notice of him.

I ambled along and more more slowly, feeling utterly wretched, but determined not to make the first advance anyway. He'd been hopelessly in the wrong. As for that wretched old Cæsar, the first time I caught him alone I'd——

King George sat down on a seat in the grounds and patted his knee twice.

I did so want to be stately and standoffish and pay him out, but it was no good. I just bounced towards him, my whole body wriggling with delight.

"Here, Happy, old boy, I want to talk to you," he said quietly in that voice I love so much.

My tail almost broke off in trying to wag further than it could. I licked his hand again and again.

Of course by this time I knew I'd behaved abominably. I couldn't live another hour unless I was sure he'd forgiven me. I rubbed my nose harder and harder against his leg, and when he gave my ear a little twist and said, "There, old chap, that's all right," I jumped right into the air three times, higher every time, happier than I had ever been before.

Then I sat down facing him, ready for the first move in our game, when he pushes his foot over a stone pretending to see if he can dislodge it from the walk without the gardener noticing it afterwards. My tail brushed the gravel to and fro. I wish I could control my tail, but I can't.  A few minutes before it had been hanging down most woefully and I *couldn't* get it to wag or to stand up anyhow, and now nothing would keep it still.

King George looked at me steadily, right in the eyes, looked at me as if he did not see me. I began to sniff at his feet to remind him it was time to find that stone.

"Happy," he said very quietly, and his voice was curious, as if he were speaking to himself, "the King cannot be quite like other men, and I suppose they'll expect something different of the King's dog, too. I'm beginning to understand the beginning of what it means to be a King, and you've got to understand too, little man."

My tail didn't wag so fast at that, but I tried to look sympathetic, for I saw he was bothered.

Someone came hurrying from the Palace.

"No time, now, Happy, to teach you. You can learn well enough if you like. Go and talk to Cæsar. *His* master understood better than anyone else, and he had no secrets from his little dog."

King George left me—how I hate this wretched "business of State" that will always interfere with our games. Any sensible dog will tell you that it's much more important to find a really good, round, right-sized stone than to sign any number of musty papers.

I was just thinking of starting a bit of fun on my own with a stake the gardener had carefully placed against some precious plant in one of the beds when I heard a funny little voice quite close to me squeak out, "Are you Happy, the King's dog?"

"I ought to have been called Miserable," I growled out. "But who on earth are you?"

"I'm the little Bird," the silly piping voice replied, "the little Bird who knows everyone, overhears everything and repeats everything interesting to everyone interested, and, if you please, I want to talk to you."

I was so amazed that I let

go of the stake and flopped right down on top of a wallflower. Perched on a rose bush just above me was a strange-looking black plumed bird with a funny wizened face and very large sparkling beady eyes. "How on earth or in the air," I asked, "did you learn to talk dog?"

"Everybody can understand me," the small voice chirped, "I speak every language. Haven't you heard people everywhere say 'a little Bird told me'? Well, the little Bird —that's me. I say, do you know the Queen?"

"Of course," I answered proudly. "I'm Happy, the King's dog."

"Well, I want you to take Her a message from 'a little Bird'—you know I get all sorts of people, humans and animals, to carry the news I hear as I fly about the world.

"The parliament of birds has just been sitting on the telegraph wires outside the Palace, and I've been deputed to wish Queen Mary a long and happy reign."

"Another of these tiresome

deputations," I growled under my breath. "Well, well, I'll take your dutiful message to Her Majesty," I said in my best court manner.

"But would you ask her too, oh! most gracious Happy"—a very well brought-up bird, I thought to myself—"if she can spare one moment in these busy times to give a thought to those most humble subjects of hers in far-off lands, whose beautiful white plumage is so cruelly torn off at the time when they need it most, just to adorn humans' heads and hats. We birds know that many of us were created to be killed for man's pleasure and woman's adornment, but if Queen Mary only said the word—she's a mother, you know, and will understand."

"I will see to it," I said. "I will inform Queen Mary."—I hadn't the least idea what the little Bird was talking about, but he seemed a polite fellow and most genuinely troubled.

"And do you think you could put in a word or two for the linnets, larks and thrushes in tiny cages?" the little voice pleaded, "and will she please ask sportsmen to try and shoot very straight, to shoot as King George shoots. We know we're made to be shot at. If only we might die quickly we should be so grateful."

I thought it was time I returned to my Palace. This little chap talked so fast I got an ache between my ears. It's an awful responsibility to be the King's dog. As I trotted back the little Bird followed me, flying and hopping from bush to bush, his head held sideways to catch the least sound, his big black eyes gleaming.

"You might ask your friends, the young Princes, too, to say a word about birds-nesting. We know our eggs are so beautiful that some must be taken away, but there are boys who don't understand that we've any feelings at all, that's the trouble," the little bird piped as I entered the Palace.

"People don't understand, or I'm sure they'd never wear ospreys or dye our feathers some horrible colour for their hats, as if God hadn't done His best to make us lovely as we are, or coop us up in tiny cages or rob us of the joys and sorrows of our nests. People don't understand, or they'd never be so cruel as to——"

I shivered as I entered the Palace. The poor little fellow was evidently troubled. I couldn't make out what was the matter. I have chased these cheeky birds off my lawn many a time, but I can't say I've ever imagined they'd any feelings like we dogs have. But we're not as unkind to them as cats are, anyway! I hate cats. Just fancy if cats and birds both have feelings. Oh! It's a most puzzling world. I'll talk to Queen Mary. She's so kind I'm sure she'll understand.

Cæsar was sitting in front of the fire when I got back. That's my place by rights, for he is only here as a visitor. I was just going to give him a shove out of the way when something about his back made me stop.

Cæsar used to be the smartest, spryest dog, always on the alert, but there he was sitting almost on the middle of his back, all huddled up, his ears limp, his head hanging down.

I thought at first he was asleep, for I've noticed as we get older we seem to be able to sleep the clock round as long as there's a fire to dream by. But he didn't move, so it couldn't be that, for he always sways slowly to one side when he's dozing, sways until he's just going to lose his balance, when he jerks quickly upright again.

"Moping," I said to myself. I gave him a friendly poke with my nose to cheer him up.

"I say, old boy, you've got the hump with a vengeance. Come on out, and I'll race you for the best mutton-bone you've ever gnawed. This Palace is so fearfully tidy that there doesn't seem to be an old shoe any-where or we'd have a tug of war. I'm sorry," I added, thinking it would please King George if I made it up with him, "I'm sorry I upset you just now. I didn't mean anything, you know—just my fun, you see." It wasn't exactly fun altogether really, but then I thought that was the right thing to say.

"Shut up!" said Cæsar. "I was just the same myself. I don't blame you a bit. I understand."

"You too?" I said. "Do *you* understand? Where did you learn it?"

"From Master,—my dear, dead Master," said Cæsar.

"Master,—my dear, dead Master, King Edward,—always understood. That was why every human and every animal loved him. People came to him with all their worries—the whole nation came. He couldn't always help, but he always understood just how they felt and that comforted them. I used to come to him myself when things had gone wrong, and when I was in a bad temper, when I was feeling neglected, and the moment he saw me he'd say, 'I understand, little doggie. You're sick of being kept indoors, or, that pointed nose of yours is a bit out of joint,' and then I felt all right again, for I knew that he'd not forget, and when he had time he'd put things right."

"But don't all humans understand?" I asked. "I thought that was the difference between them and us."

"Do they?" said Cæsar bitterly. "You're very young, Happy, and not over observant. Why, they don't begin to understand animals, let alone each other."

"I remember."—Oh my! I thought to myself, I'm in for it now, but I suppose a King's dog must try to look interested even when he is most utterly bored.—"I remember once going in the car to call with Master at some big house. It was a very hot day, and I was enjoying the sunshine so much that I thought I wouldn't go in with him but wait on the seat till he came out, and look at the people who were passing. A beautiful carriage drove up and stopped beside us, and two beautiful ladies got out. A beautiful fat coachman sat on the box behind two of the grandest horses I have ever seen. I was watching the ladies and thinking those horses were in luck's way to have such a home, when I heard them noisily jangling away at their harness and viciously munching at their bits.

"I got my paws on the window ledge and screwed my head round to have a look at them and see what was up. I couldn't for the life of me make out the look in their eyes. They were bloodshot and strained and half mad, as if they were being tortured. Yet the beautiful fat old coachman seemed perfectly happy and most grandfatherly.

"And then I understood.

"The poor beasts were curbed up till every muscle in their shining necks stood out like knotted whips. The flies were buzzing round their ears and noses. Some had settled on that tender part close to their lips which feels so soft that I love to get old Kildare to

nibble at me in his stall so that
I can feel it. It's just like the
very best velvet, like the dress
*She* wears sometimes, and
which I always press close
against whenever I get a chance
—'You do love the feel of
panne, Cæsar, don't you?'
*She*'ll say when I'm afraid of
creasing it.

"Well, would you believe it,
those poor things could hardly
move their heads an inch without agony, yet they flung them
up and down and rocked them
to and fro to try and get rid of
the flies, and actually stamped

holes in the pavement in the hope they'd crush a fly or two, while the fat old coachman didn't seem to notice or care. Their tongues were beginning to loll out between their teeth, there was froth round their mouths. When Master came out with the ladies I was so angry I barked and growled at them.

" 'Be quiet, Cæsar,' he said, 'they're friends of mine.'

"But I just barked and growled all the louder. As they drove off and he turned towards the car, he saw what had made me so angry, and a look of real suffering came over his face.

"'The kindest women in London, Cæsar,' he said, 'but they don't understand.'"

I didn't quite see why Cæsar should do all the talking. He's getting very garrulous in his old age—he's not old really but he's gone through a lot—so I yawned a mighty yawn, which is the right way of drawing attention to yourself.

"For the matter of that," I said, "it's not so easy to find people who understand little dogs either. If only they'd explain what they wanted us to do, and why they wanted us to do it, and talk to us nicely, we dogs, you know, are always only too anxious to do the right thing. Well perhaps that *is* a slight exaggeration, but really I do believe we're always willing to understand, even if we don't always quite see our way to obey. The trouble of it is so few have the patience to explain."

Cæsar was'nt taking the least notice of me. That's the worst of him now. He always seems taken up with his own thoughts.

He lives in the past, I suppose.

I'm too excited about the present to remember any past at all.

So although I yawned again and gave a huge sigh and a mighty sniff, he went steadily on:

"Master was silent all the way home. He hardly spoke at dinner. He gave me my usual bone without a word, but a bone did not taste the same unless he teased me a bit first and said, when at last he let me take it, 'There you are, you young rascal, you don't deserve it but I suppose we can't let you starve.' People came and went all the evening, important people with serious faces. They talked and talked. And then Master talked, and they shook their heads and looked more solemn. I found them very tiresome and I badly wanted them to go. Master talked again, and in the end I saw them begin to get less serious, and one smiled and said, 'It's settled then, Sir, that you will go.'

"'Of course,' said Master. 'I think I understand them a little, and they understand me. A cordial understanding is worth all the treaties in the world, isn't it?'

"At last we were alone, and Master lit his big cigar, and drew his chair to the fire. I jumped up beside him, pushed his coat a bit on one side, tucked my head under his arm, and put my paws across his knees.

"'Well, old man,' he said, 'that's settled anyway. I do wish people would try and understand each other a bit better. It would save such a lot of trouble, such a lot of waste of blood and money.'

"I suppose I looked rather surprised, for I, too, thought humans always understood each other.

"'My dear little doggie,' he said, 'I believe nearly all the trouble in this world comes through misunderstanding.'

"Then he repeated something in French that I've heard him say many a time when he's been worried. Unfortunately my French isn't what it might be, though I've certainly travelled enough in France with Master. As a matter of fact I rather despised French ways and French dogs and the silly French language that they seem to understand just as well as I do English, till Master compelled me to make friends with that French poodle at Biarritz, and then I was sorry I'd not made better use of my opportunities.

"'To understand everything is to forgive everything,' Master said slowly. 'If only people remembered that, diplomacy would be child's play, and they'd have no need of a Peacemaker. But they *will* misunderstand meanings and motives, they will *not* put themselves in the other man's place, they will *not* look at things from the other fellow's point of view.'

"'And,' he laughed that deep, rich laugh of his, 'they sometimes think I'm going too far in search of the other man's place and the other fellow's point of view. But I'm not, Cæsar, *I'm not*, I tell you. I'm going to make the nations understand each other a little better before I die. I know the fault is not all ours, but we must lead the way—*I* must lead the way. Go to sleep, old man. I've work to do.'"

I really was beginning to weary a little of all this. To tell the truth, though I wouldn't admit it to Cæsar for a moment, it is a bit above my head as yet, for I've only been the King's dog a very short time. And so I thought I'd end the matter by saying,

"Well, as your Master understood so much, and you were with him so long, perhaps you'll explain why he's not here still, and why I'm the King's dog and not you."

"No," said Cæsar very, very sadly, and his head, which had brisked up as he talked of his Master, hung low again, "I don't understand. How I wish I did. If only I could be with him just for one evening perhaps he would explain, but I am afraid there are some things little dogs can never, never understand."

"Does *She?*" I whispered. We always still speak of *Her* in whispers, for *Her* sorrow is so great.

"Sometimes," said Cæsar, wrinkling his forehead, "I think *She* does—not everything, perhaps, but a great, great deal. There *must* be Some One somewhere, Who knows and understands everything, and I am sure He has told *Her* and explained. But *She* can't tell me, although *She*'s tried. I wonder, oh, I wonder, if some day I *shall* understand. I'd so gladly die to-morrow if only I could understand."

My name and nature is Happy, you know, and I can't be serious for long at a time, I'm afraid.

"Well," I said cheerfully, "If *I* were King George, I'd just *make* everyone understand."

"You can't do it that way," Cæsar replied, "you've got to persuade them ever so slowly, and teach them ever so carefully.

Very few people know how to
do it, and everything depends on
how it's done. I've heard Master say that lots of times."

"Will King George know the
way?" I asked anxiously.

"Of course," said Cæsar,
quite sharply. "Master will
have told him. He's Master's
son, you see."

PRINTED IN THE CITY OF LONDON
AT THE EDINBURGH PRESS